Flame

The air began to shimmer, and Chloe saw swirls of pink glitter falling around her.

"Ow!" she exclaimed as specks flew into her face. "What's that?"

She looked down and saw grains of sand dusting the pommel of the saddle. "Sand?" she muttered, brushing it away with her hand. "I can't be imagining *that*!"

The glitter began to clear, and she tried to grab on to the twisty golden pole again – but it had disappeared! Instead, her hands landed on a soft, silky mane. What was going on? She wasn't sitting on a carousel at all now. Flame was a real, live pony!

Also available
Sparkle
Brightheart
Star
Jewel
Crystal

Flame

Poppy Shire

Illustrated by Strawberrie Donnelly

MACMILLAN CHILDREN'S BOOKS

A Working Partners Book

With special thanks to Gill Harvey

First published 2006 by Macmillan Children's Books
a division of Macmillan Publishers Limited
20 New Wharf Road, London N1 9RR
Basingstoke and Oxford
www.panmacmillan.com

Associated companies throughout the world

ISBN-13: 978-0-330-44598-6
ISBN-10: 0-330-44598-7

Text copyright © Working Partners Limited 2006
Illustrations copyright © Strawberrie Donnelly 2006

Created by Working Partners Limited

1 3 5 7 9 8 6 4 2

A CIP catalogue record for this book is available from
the British Library.

Printed and bound in Great Britain by
Mackays of Chatham plc, Kent

Contents

1. A Special Trip to the Fair

The fairground looked lovely in the misty morning light. It was in Chloe's local park, at the bottom of a hill. She gazed down on the colourful rides in delight as she and her dad made their way to the entrance.

"Come on – let's find an exciting ride!" she cried as soon as they were inside the gates.

"Don't you want to get some candyfloss first?" her dad asked.

Chloe loved candyfloss! She was about to say yes, but one of the rides suddenly caught her eye. She gasped.

"*Barker's Magic Pony Carousel*," she read out loud.

The carousel was painted in red, gold and silver swirls, and the beautiful wooden ponies rose gracefully up and down under rows of twinkling lights. Chloe couldn't tear her eyes away!

"Is that a no then?" teased her dad.

"Do you think I could have some candyfloss *after* trying the carousel?" Chloe said.

"Oh, I should think so," her dad said, ruffling her hair. "Why don't you go and get on board? We can find a candyfloss stall afterwards."

"Thanks, Dad," Chloe said happily. She didn't have any brothers or sisters to play with, but her dad made sure that she never felt lonely. He was always taking her to do fun things, like visiting this fairground, and at home they liked reading mysterious detective stories together.

She skipped over to the carousel to choose a pony. The ride had just slowed to a halt, and one pony seemed to be gazing right at her. She was a stunning golden Arabian pony with a creamy mane and tail and beautiful big brown eyes. Chloe knew she must be an Arabian pony because she looked like she'd cantered straight out of the desert!

She ran forward for a closer look. The pony's saddle was covered in deep ruby-red velvet with golden studs around the edge. There were matching studs decorating the bridle. The ruby saddlecloth was embroidered in the colours of a desert sunset, with a border of shiny golds, and a fringe of pink and purple tassels all around the edge.

"Wow!" Chloe exclaimed. At her local riding school, she loved helping to get ponies ready for shows. She wasn't a very confident rider yet, but she was really good at plaiting manes and weaving pretty ribbons into the hair. She looked closely at the gorgeous saddlecloth. Whoever had made this must love decorating ponies as much as she did!

"Hello there!" said a deep, friendly voice. Chloe whirled around and saw a tall man stepping down from the carousel. He was wearing a red velvet suit lined with green silk and a stripy red and green top hat.

"Hello," said Chloe. "Are you Mr Barker?"

"I am indeed!" said the man, his eyes sparkling. "Would you like to ride on my splendid carousel?"

Chloe nodded. "Yes, please. I'd like to ride the Arabian pony, if that's OK."

Mr Barker stroked his chin. "Well, that's fine by me," he said, "but we'll have to see what the carousel thinks."

"The carousel?" Chloe was puzzled.

Mr Barker tapped his nose and leaned towards her. "It's a *magic* carousel, remember!" he whispered. Then he reached out and took a bright orange balloon from a passing balloon seller.

With a flourish, he pulled a little pony-shaped badge out of his lapel. "Now, Chloe, let's see if your wish will come true!"

Before Chloe had time to wonder how Mr Barker could possibly know her name, he burst the balloon with the badge pin. *POP!* Chloe stared in amazement as a little pink ticket fluttered to the ground.

Mr Barker beamed at her. "I think you'll find there's something written on it," he said.

Chloe could just see some swirly silver writing on one side of the ticket. She bent down to pick it up. "*Flame,*" she read, then looked up at Mr Barker hopefully.

"What a coincidence!" he said with a wink.

Chloe ran over to the Arabian pony.

There was a name written on her pretty red headband. She stood on tiptoe to read it.

"Flame!" she exclaimed.

2. Deserted!

"All aboard!" cried Mr Barker. "Roll up, roll up for the most exciting ride of your lives! The Magic Pony Carousel is about to start!"

Quickly Chloe scrambled up on to Flame's back. She had read books about different kinds of ponies, and she knew a lot about Arabians. Chloe knew that they came from the desert, where they had to be strong and fast to race long distances over the sand.

She patted Flame's shiny wooden neck,

8

then held on tight to the twisty golden pole. The carousel began to turn, lifting her gently up and down. Chloe pictured what it would be like to ride across the desert with the sun beating down. She could almost feel the warm rays on her skin . . . But then the air began to shimmer, and Chloe saw swirls of pink glitter falling around her. She rubbed her eyes. She must be imagining things! But no – the glitter was still falling softly.

"Ow!" she exclaimed as specks flew into her face. "What's that?"

She looked down and saw grains of sand dusting the pommel of the saddle. "Sand?" she muttered, brushing it away with her hand. "I can't be imagining *that*!"

The glitter began to clear, and she tried to grab on to the twisty golden pole again –

but it had disappeared! Instead, her hands landed on a soft, silky mane. Chloe nearly fell out of the saddle in surprise. Hastily she steadied herself on the saddle's high pommel and picked up the red leather reins. What was going on? She wasn't sitting on a carousel at all now. Flame was a real, live pony!

The fairground had vanished. Instead, there was golden shimmering sand everywhere, as far as she could see. She and Flame were galloping through the rolling dunes of a desert.

"Steady!" cried Chloe. She had never ridden this fast before! She gave a little tug on the reins and felt Flame slow down to a canter. The sand was still flying into her face, so Chloe groped for the pocket of her fleecy pink cardigan, looking for a handkerchief to hold over her nose. To her astonishment the pocket wasn't there. She glanced down. She wasn't wearing her cardigan at all!

Chloe was wearing a pale blue cotton gown embroidered with pretty yellow cross stitches. There was a little kerchief around her neck in rich sky blue, decorated with a fringe of tiny red and blue beads. Chloe quickly lifted it up to cover her nose and mouth. It kept the sand out perfectly. Then she reached up and patted her hair. Phew! She was still wearing her favourite hairclip decorated with rainbow-coloured butter-flies. This was all very mysterious, but exciting, too!

As Flame's hoofs thudded across the golden sand dunes, Chloe saw that they were approaching a little town. All the houses were whitewashed, and many of them had

domed roofs that stood out against the deep
blue sky. In the brilliant sunshine they were
almost too bright to look at. Chloe shaded
her eyes with one hand as Flame slowed
down to a trot.

They reached the edge of the town and
trotted down a narrow street. Chloe spotted
a man leading a donkey laden with baskets
of vegetables. She reined Flame to a walk

and followed the donkey over the smooth, shiny cobbles. The street opened into a square with palm trees in the middle, surrounding a stone well. All around the edge of the square were colourful, busy market stalls.

"Wow!" said Chloe. "What a great place!"

"Yes, isn't it?" agreed a voice.

Chloe looked around, wondering who had spoken. There wasn't anyone nearby. With a shrug, she nudged Flame forward, looking at the different market stalls. There were richly woven rugs and hangings, mounds of scented spices, wonderful fabrics and clothes.

"Figs! Lovely plump figs!" called one stallholder. He smiled at Chloe and held one out to her.

13

She laughed and shook her head. The fig looked delicious but she didn't have any money.

A woman wearing a bright red shawl walked past with a jug of water balanced on her head. The sight of the crystal clear water made Chloe realize how thirsty she was.

"Oh! I'd love a drink," she exclaimed out loud.

"So would I!"

It was the mysterious voice again! Chloe peered around, but no one seemed to be taking any notice of her. Shaking her head in puzzlement, she slipped down from Flame's back and led her over to the palm trees beside the well. She lifted the reins over Flame's head and tied her to a wooden post.

"I won't be a minute, Flame," she told

her, patting her golden neck. Then she headed towards the well. A group of girls were waiting with stone jars for their turn to draw water.

"Hey!" called the voice again.

Chloe spun around. There was no one behind her, just Flame tied to the post.

"Please could I have a drink too?" begged the voice. "It was very hot galloping across the desert!"

Chloe stared hard. Could it be . . . ? She stepped forward. "Flame," she whispered, "was that you?"

The pony blinked her big brown eyes. "Of course it was!" she said.

Chloe flung her arms around Flame's neck. "You can talk!" she cried. "This is the best carousel ride ever!"

Flame nuzzled her cheek. "I can talk, but

you picked the ticket with my name on it, so only you can understand me," she said. "The carousel has sent us here to help someone and sort out a problem. I'm not sure what it is yet though. We'll have to find that out for ourselves."

Chloe had a worrying thought. "What about my dad? He won't know where I've gone!"

Flame shook her long silky mane. "Don't worry," she said. "We're in magic time here. When we get back, it will be as if we've never been away."

"Wow!" breathed Chloe. "My very own magical adventure with my very own Arabian pony!"

"That's right," agreed Flame. "A very *thirsty* Arabian pony!"

3. Chloe Makes Some Friends
— and a Foe

Chloe untied the reins and led Flame over
to the well. She smiled shyly at the girls.
Three of them were chatting together and
they smiled back. But the fourth girl didn't
look up from filling her water jar. They all
wore colourful gowns like the one that
Chloe was wearing. She loved the bright
orange gown worn by the girl closest to her.

An elderly woman finished filling her jar
and offered Chloe a chance to use the
bucket that had to be lowered into the well.

Chloe pushed it over the edge of the stone wall and listened to it splash into the water below. Then she pulled on the rope. Slowly the bucket came up, full of sparkling water. She reached out to grab hold of the bucket and began to pull it over the side of the well, but it was heavier than she expected. The bucket slipped from her fingers and sloshed cold water all over the girl in the beautiful orange gown!

"Oh!" gasped the girl.

"I'm so sorry!" Chloe exclaimed.

But the girl was laughing. She had warm brown eyes and long dark hair that gleamed in the sun. "Don't worry!" she said. "It's nice and cool!"

She helped Chloe put the bucket on the ground. As she bent down, the girl dipped the tips of her fingers into the bucket and flicked water over Chloe's hair.

Chloe shook her head and felt drops of water trickle down her neck. The girl was right – it did feel nice and cool. Then she reached into the bucket and splashed the girl back! The girl yelped and began to run around the well. Laughing, Chloe chased after her new friend until she dived behind two of the other girls.

"Come on, you two, protect me!" she

begged, peeping out from between them as Chloe approached.

"You're joking, Mina!" they exclaimed. One of them reached into her own bucket and flicked more water over Mina's orange gown. Mina squealed and ran off again. The other girls helped Chloe to chase her. They were soon gasping with laughter.

"Hanna, help me!" Mina called to the fourth girl.

The fourth girl frowned and shook her head.

Mina tried to hide behind Flame.

The pony stuck her nose into the bucket of water. "Watch this," she said to Chloe.

As Mina crept forward to peep under Flame's neck, the pony suddenly lifted her head out of the bucket, splashing *all* the girls, even Chloe.

"Flame!" Chloe squealed. "You weren't supposed to get me too. I'm *soaked*!"

Flame snorted and looked around with wide, innocent eyes.

Mina laughed. "She meant to do it, I'm sure she did!"

Chloe put her arm around Flame's neck and smiled at her new friends. "This is Flame," she said. "And I'm Chloe. Do you have ponies too?"

Mina nodded. "Yes, but they're at home. My pony's name is Flicker and I'm Mina."

"I'm Amira and this is my sister Nadia," said another of the girls. She picked up her water jar. "We'd better get going, Nadia."

"OK," said Nadia. "Nice to meet you, Chloe."

Mina waved as they walked out of the square, then turned to the fourth girl, who was still standing beside the well. "This is my best friend, Hanna," she told Chloe.

Chloe watched as Hanna balanced her water jar on top of her head and walked gracefully towards them. "*Another* new friend, Mina? I have to go, my mum's waiting for me," Hanna snapped. "Are you coming or not?"

"I just wanted you to meet Chloe," said Mina. She hesitated. Chloe hoped she would stay by the well. She liked Mina a lot, and she didn't know anyone else here.

Mina picked up her water jar. "I haven't filled my jar yet," she said. "I'll follow you in a minute."

Hanna gave a little shrug and walked off. Chloe thought she was acting very oddly. Mina was so nice, but Hanna didn't seem friendly at all!

"Maybe she was feeling left out," Flame whispered in Chloe's ear.

Chloe stroked Flame's neck and nodded. That might make sense.

"Bye, Hanna!" called Mina, but her friend didn't turn round.

Mina's face fell, and Chloe felt sorry for her. But then Mina grinned. "I think Hanna needs her ears testing," she joked. "Never mind. I'll see her later. Let's take this water home and you can meet Flicker."

Mina started leading the way across the square. "Are you visiting for our pageant?"

"Pageant? Oh – yes," Chloe stuttered. Whatever the pageant was, it sounded fun.

And it obviously gave her a good reason to be visiting the town. She could hardly tell Mina that she'd been transported here by magic!

"I thought you must be," said Mina. "Flame has such a gorgeous saddlecloth. Did you make it yourself?"

"No. I wish I had though," Chloe answered truthfully. She wished Mina would stop asking awkward questions!

To her relief, Mina was distracted by one of the stallholders. She seemed to know everyone! All the people they met were very friendly. They patted Flame's neck as Chloe led her behind Mina, but her pony didn't seem to mind. In fact, Chloe thought she looked rather pleased to be getting so much attention!

Mina turned down another street and

then another. There were chickens pecking in the dust, and a goat tethered to a ring in the wall. People left their doors wide open and Chloe peeked in as they passed. Inside the shadowy houses, women sat chatting cross-legged on colourful mats. The men seemed to prefer sitting outside, gathering at street corners to drink little glasses of black tea.

"It's not far now," said Mina. "I can't wait to show you my saddlecloth. I've been working on it for days!"

"You've made your own?" exclaimed Chloe. "What colour is it?"

"Bright blue silk," said Mina proudly. "With lots of gold and silver stitching."

"That sounds lovely," said Chloe.

Mina smiled at her. "It's almost finished – I've just got a tiny bit of stitching left to do.

I don't have any brothers or sisters, so Hanna's been helping me to finish it off."

Chloe knew exactly what it felt like, being an only child. "I don't have any brothers or sisters either," she admitted. "But friends are just as good!"

Mina nodded. "That's what I think too," she agreed. Then her face clouded over and she frowned. "But it's odd. Hanna's been grumpy lately," she said. "I know she's shy, but she's not usually this quiet. I can't work out what's wrong."

Chloe didn't know what to say. Hanna hadn't been very friendly towards her, but she was still Mina's best friend!

Mina turned one more corner and pointed to a house at the end of the street. "That's where I live," she said. "And there's the stable next to it."

The house was so pretty! Its mud-brick walls were whitewashed and a beautiful dome formed part of the roof. They entered a courtyard through an archway with patterns cut around the edge of the mud-brick. Bright pink flowers grew around the arch, dazzling splashes of colour against the white paint.

Mina put the water jar down next to a doorway.

"I'm home!" she called into the house before leading the way across the courtyard to the stable. "I expect Flame's tired," Mina said. "She can rest in the stall next to Flicker for a while."

"That sounds like a good idea!" Flame whispered in Chloe's ear. "Mina could be the person we're supposed to help. The stable might give us some clues."

28

Chloe stroked Flame's soft nose and straightened her creamy gold forelock. "Maybe there'll be some nice hay too," she whispered back.

Mina opened the stable door and was greeted with a friendly whinny. "Hello, Flicker!" she said to a pretty chestnut pony. "I've brought you a friend. Say hello to Flame!"

Chloe led Flame into the stall and slipped her bridle off. The ponies looked at each other with their ears pricked, then touched noses and blew softly at each other.

"They're going to get on perfectly!" Mina laughed. "Come on, let's go to the tack room. I'm *dying* to show you my saddlecloth!"

She skipped through another doorway, with Chloe close behind her. But the moment she stepped inside the tack room, Mina let out a wail.

"Oh no!" she cried. "It's *ruined*!"

4. A Sabotaged Saddlecloth

"What's happened?" Chloe asked. She peered over Mina's shoulder. A square of blue silk was lying crumpled on the floor.

Mina stepped forward and picked it up.

"Look!" she sobbed. "Someone's completely wrecked it!"

Chloe stared at the saddlecloth in dismay. The lovely blue cloth was covered in mud and dust, and there were rips and tears all over the fabric. Worst of all, the beautiful silver and gold embroidery that had taken Mina so long was all picked loose.

"How *awful*," Chloe said in a trembling voice. "Who would do something so horrible?"

"I don't know," Mina sobbed. "But there's no way I'll be able to join in the pageant now."

Chloe put an arm around her. Surely there was something she could do to help?

"Could you help her make another one, Chloe?" whinnied Flame, who was watching through the door.

Chloe stared at the ruined saddlecloth. It might just be possible. "Mina, when exactly is the pageant? I've forgotten," she said.

"Tomorrow afternoon," Mina sniffed, dropping the saddlecloth to the floor. "It's too late to do anything now."

Chloe shook her head. "No it isn't," she said. "I can sew too. If we both work really hard, we could make a new one. Where did you buy the cloth and the thread?"

"The market," Mina said, sounding more hopeful. "It'll be closing soon though . . . "

"But it's still open now, isn't it?" said Chloe.

Mina nodded.

"Then wait here," Chloe ordered. She ran back into the stable and took Flame's bridle off its hook. Hurriedly she slipped it over her pony's ears. "You're right, Flame," she whispered. "I need to help Mina make a new saddlecloth. Can you remember the way back to the market?"

"Of course I can!" said Flame, tossing her head. "Let's go!"

Chloe scrambled up on to Flame's back and they trotted out of the courtyard.

"We won't be long!" Chloe called over her shoulder to Mina.

Flame set off along the winding streets. Chloe clung on tight to the saddle – with all the twisting and turning, she was worried she'd fall off! And she was glad Flame had such a good sense of direction, because she soon felt completely lost.

"Look – there's a tea glass on the ground. That's where those men were drinking tea," Flame puffed, and turned right.

Chloe caught a glimpse of the glass as they cantered past.

"And there's one of the goats we passed before," said the pony, pointing her nose to where a black and white goat was tethered. "We're almost there!"

"Well done, Flame!" Chloe gasped as they clattered into the market square. "Now all we have to do is find the fabric stall."

Some of the stallholders were already packing up. "Oh *please* let the fabric stall still be here!" Chloe pleaded out loud.

"Are you looking for me?" called a cheerful voice. Chloe twisted around in the saddle – and there, just behind her, was a stall overflowing with the most beautiful fabrics she'd ever seen! There were rolls of cloth in all colours of the rainbow – bright reds and yellows, brilliant greens and deep, luscious purples.

Chloe slid down from the saddle. "I'm so glad I've found you!" she exclaimed. "My friend Mina bought her fabric and threads from you to make her saddlecloth. But now it's been ruined and we have to make another one in double-quick time. The only trouble is, I'm not even sure which fabric she bought . . . " she finished, looking hopefully

at the stallholder, who was wearing a gorgeous red waistcoat.

The man smiled. He had lovely sparkling eyes and as Chloe stared at him, her mouth dropped open. He looked just like Mr Barker from the Magic Pony Carousel!

"Oh yes, I know Mina," he said. "And I remember what she bought too." He started lifting several rolls of fabric out of the way. "Now, where is it?" he muttered. "Ah! I think it was this one." He pulled out a roll of silky blue fabric.

"That's right!" Chloe said.

"She used this to make it soft for Flicker's back," he went on, pulling out a roll of thick grey-blue felt, "and this thread." He pulled a box from underneath the stall and picked out a reel of silver thread. Then he scratched his head. "Now, where's that gold thread?"

Chloe watched anxiously as he hunted for the gold thread. At last the stallholder shook his head and held up an empty reel. "I'm sorry. I've sold it all, I'm afraid," he said.

"Oh dear," said Chloe. The saddlecloth wouldn't be the same without the gold!

"I have plenty of green and blue thread," the stallholder offered.

Chloe shook her head. Those colours wouldn't show up very well on the blue fabric. "Never mind," she said. "The blue cloth and silver thread will have to do."

She watched as he wrapped them in paper, and tried not to feel too disappointed about the gold thread. The silver will look lovely on its own, she told herself.

Suddenly Chloe's heart skipped a beat. How could she have been so silly? She hadn't got any money! She'd left Mina in such a hurry that she'd forgotten to ask for some. *Now* what was she going to do?

The stallholder handed her the parcel. "I–I'm sorry," Chloe stammered. "I've made a horrible mistake . . . You see, I don't have any . . . "

The man smiled, looking more like Mr. Barker than ever. "Now, don't you worry," he said. "I know Mina's family very well. They can pay me tomorrow."

Chloe breathed a big sigh of relief. "Thank you!" she cried. She took the parcel and turned to climb back into the saddle.

"Wait a minute," said the man. "Before you go, there's one more thing . . . " He held up a little woven bag. "I'm sure you can think of something to do with these."

Chloe peeped into the bag, then gasped

39

in delight. The bag was full of thick silk ribbons, all in different colours. "They're perfect!" she cried. "I'll be able to weave them into Flame and Flicker's manes, just like I do at the riding school!"

"I thought you'd find them useful," said the stallholder with a wink.

Chloe climbed back into the saddle and waved goodbye. Flame set off at a brisk canter and Chloe grabbed the pommel with one hand, holding her parcels tight with the other.

"Good luck!" the man called after her.

5. Preparing for the Pageant

As they drew closer to Mina's house, Chloe began to feel worried. "What if Mina's really upset about the gold thread?" she wondered. "She might not want to make a saddlecloth without it."

"Well, we've done our best," said Flame. "The silver will look nice."

"But she was so proud of all that gold stitching," Chloe said sadly.

Flame slowed to a trot as they turned the corner into Mina's street. Suddenly she stopped dead.

"What is it?" Chloe asked in alarm.

"I've just had an idea!" Flame whinnied. "You could use some strands of my tail instead of gold thread. They look very shiny in the sun."

"That's a brilliant idea!" Chloe leaned down and hugged Flame's neck. "Come on, let's tell Mina!"

They found Mina sitting in the courtyard with the saddlecloth in her lap, picking at the ruined stitches. She looked up anxiously as Flame and Chloe rode in.

"Did you get everything?" she asked.

Chloe slid down to the ground and showed Mina the bag of fabric and thread. "*Nearly* everything," she said. "There wasn't any gold thread left."

Mina's face fell. "No gold thread!"

"But I've got an idea," Chloe went on.

She knew she had to pretend it was her own idea — Mina would never believe she had a talking pony! "We could use some hairs from Flame's tail instead."

Mina looked at Flame's flowing golden tail and smiled. She stood up and planted a kiss on Flame's soft muzzle. "Let's get started at once. My mum's given us a picnic dinner so that we can stay in the stable to make the new saddlecloth. Look!" She picked up a reed basket.

It reminded Chloe of the woven bag. "And look what the stallholder gave me too!" She pulled out a handful of shiny ribbons to show Mina. "I can weave them into our ponies' manes."

"Perfect," said Mina. "Everything's going to be all right, isn't it?"

"Of course it is!" Chloe agreed.

The two girls took everything into the stable, and settled Flame back next to Flicker. Mina shooed her fluffy black cat out of the hay store so they could each make a soft pile to sit on. The cat watched them, licking its paws, as they snuggled into the hay and started work. It was such a cosy place to be that it didn't feel like work at all!

First, they stitched the silk on to the felt underside. Then Mina explained how she'd made pretty patterns with the thread.

"Let's do the silver part first," she said. "We can weave the golden parts in afterwards, with strands of Flame's tail."

"All right," Chloe said. "I'll start at the opposite end so we meet in the middle."

The girls worked in silence at first, concentrating hard. After a while, Mina looked up. "Are you hungry yet?" she asked.

Just then, Chloe's tummy rumbled, and they both laughed.

"I think that's a yes!" said Mina. "Here, have some bread. My mum makes it herself. And here's hummus to dip it in, and baba ganoush – that's made with aubergines – and there's some cold lamb too."

The two girls quickly finished their meal

and filled the rack in the stable with fresh hay so their ponies could have supper too. Then they carried on with the sewing. Soon it began to get dark, so Mina fetched oil lamps for them to see by. They made the stable look really pretty, casting a gentle orangey-yellow glow on the walls and creating flickering shadows. Chloe looked at Flame, who had finished her hay and was dozing with one hind leg resting under her tummy. Her golden coat looked beautiful in the soft lamplight.

The saddlecloth was beginning to take shape, though there was a lot of stitching to do. Once the silver thread was finished, Chloe went over to Flame to pluck some of her golden tail hairs out.

"I'm trying not to hurt you," she said, as

she carefully pulled out the hairs one at a time.

"Don't worry," said Flame. "It doesn't really hurt."

Chloe ran back to Mina and showed her the hairs from Flame's tail. They shone in the lamplight, exactly like gold.

"They're beautiful," Mina said. She threaded one through her needle and frowned at the saddlecloth. "I think I'll do a bird first," she said.

Chloe threaded her own needle and joined in.

At last, Mina sewed the final stitch – the top of a golden palm tree – and held up the cloth for them to look at.

"Wow!" Chloe whispered. "I can't believe I've helped to make something so beautiful!"

Mina put the cloth down and gave her a hug. "Well, you did," she said happily. She placed the saddlecloth safely to one side and sank back on to the hay.

Chloe yawned, stretching her arms above her head. Her fingers were aching and her eyes were sore, but it had all been worth it.

"I suppose we should go back into the house," Mina said sleepily, "but it's so comfortable here . . ."

"I think I'm too tired to move," Chloe muttered. She felt her eyes closing . . . closing . . . She wriggled deeper into the soft warm hay and fell fast asleep.

She woke up with a jolt. The lamps were still burning, and it was very dark outside. Mina was asleep beside her, curled up on the hay. Chloe sat up. Something had woken her. She listened carefully, her heart beating faster. Yes – there it was again! A soft noise just outside the stable.

"Flame!" she whispered, and the pony twitched her ears to show she was awake. "Did you hear that? It sounded like footsteps."

Flame snorted. "I think I heard something," she said. She pricked up her ears, listening. "It's stopped now. Don't worry, I'll keep one ear open. You can go back to sleep."

Chloe lay back on the hay. She kept listening for a few more minutes, wondering what she could have heard. Perhaps it was Mina's mum or dad, checking that they were OK. Or perhaps it had been nothing at all. She rested her head on her arm and soon fell back to sleep.

"Wake up, Chloe!" called Mina's voice. "It's time for breakfast!"

Chloe was so comfortable that she didn't want to wake up, but Mina was shaking her shoulder. She opened her eyes. Daylight was streaming into the stable, and Flame and Flicker were munching a fresh batch of hay.

"It's pageant day!" Mina sang. "Come

on, I bet Mum will cook a delicious breakfast for us!"

Chloe rubbed her eyes. "That sounds great," she said, scrambling to her feet. "How does the saddlecloth look in daylight?"

Mina's eyes lit up. "It's *gorgeous*," she declared, holding it up.

She was right. Sunbeams danced over the silver thread and the golden strands of Flame's tail, making them glint and sparkle.

Mina put the saddlecloth down and tried to open the stable door. But it didn't move.

"That's funny," she said. "It never usually sticks!" She gave it another push. It *still* wouldn't move!

"Let me try," said Chloe. She leaned against the door and pushed with all her might. The door didn't budge one tiny bit.

"It must be locked," Mina said in dismay. "Someone's locked it from the outside!"

"That must have been what we heard in the night, Chloe," snorted Flame, who was standing behind them. "You thought it was footsteps, didn't you?"

Chloe frowned. It was hard to believe that someone would lock them in. "Could it have happened by accident?" she asked Mina.

Mina shook her head. "You have to push the bolt across. What's going on, Chloe? First my saddlecloth was ruined, and now this!" She bit her lip. "It looks as if someone doesn't want me to go to the pageant."

"I'm sure there must be another explanation," soothed Chloe. She wondered if she should tell Mina about the footsteps, but Mina seemed worried enough already. She ran her hand over her hair, trying to think of something that might help. Her hand brushed against her butterfly hairclip.

"Could you use your clip to unbolt the door?" Flame asked, watching her.

Chloe caught Flame's eye and nodded. It was worth a try. She pulled the hairclip out of her hair. "I could try sliding the bolt open with this," she said to Mina.

Mina frowned. "How?" she said. "The bolt's on the outside."

Chloe inspected the door. "Look, there's a little gap between the door and the frame. I should be able to slide the hairclip through it and push the bolt back."

She opened the clip and pushed the silver part through the gap. Then she wiggled the clip around until she could feel the end of the bolt.

Mina peered anxiously over Chloe's shoulder. "Is the bolt moving?"

Chloe wiggled the clip some more. "Yes! I just felt it slide back a little bit!"

"Keep going!" Mina said.

With a final twist of the clip, the bolt slid back and the door swung open. "Hurray!" Chloe shouted. "We did it!"

"*You* did it," Mina corrected her, giving

her a hug. "I don't know what I would have done without you!" Then her face grew serious. "But we still don't know why these horrible things have happened." She shook her head. "Why would someone want to stop me from taking part in the pageant?"

6. Chloe Hunts for Clues

"Whoever is doing these things, we'll find them," Chloe promised. "We need to pretend we're in a detective story and hunt for clues. Maybe we should go for a ride to look for suspects."

Mina nodded. "Good idea," she said. "Come on. Let's have breakfast before we start searching."

As soon as they had finished, they headed out to the stables to tack up the ponies. Flicker looked so pretty with her new saddlecloth. The blue silk and gold thread gleamed against her chestnut coat.

Chloe put on Flame's saddle and bridle, but as they were walking out of the stable the Arabian pony stopped dead in the doorway.

"What is it?" Chloe whispered.

Flame scraped her hoof on the ground. "Look down there," she said.

Chloe frowned. Flame had spotted some sunflower seeds! Just a few of them, scattered on the ground by the door.

"Mina," she said, "do you ever feed Flicker sunflower seeds?"

"No," said Mina. "Why?"

"There are some on the ground here. I don't remember seeing them yesterday. They must have been dropped by the person who locked the stable door!"

Mina stared at where Chloe was pointing.

"That's a great clue!" she said, her cheeks turning pink with excitement. "All we have to do is find someone who's been eating sunflower seeds!"

"It would be a good start," Chloe agreed.

"We should go and find Hanna," declared Mina. "She loves detective stories. She'll help us to track the culprit down!"

"I love detective stories too!" Chloe exclaimed. It was nice to find out that she and Hanna had something in common. It might make it easier to get to know her.

The two girls mounted their ponies and trotted out of the yard. "Hanna lives in the next street," said Mina.

But when they got to Hanna's house, her mother told them that she had gone for a ride in the desert with her brother.

"I know where they'll have gone," said Mina. "It won't take us long to catch them up. We can gallop fast through the dunes."

Chloe felt a bit nervous. She remembered how fast Flame had been galloping when they arrived from the carousel. Just from looking at Mina in the saddle, Chloe could tell that she was a much better rider. She hoped she'd be able to keep up without falling off!

"Don't worry," said Flame, as if she knew what Chloe was thinking. "I'll look after you!"

Mina led the way through the winding streets until they reached the edge of the town. Miles of golden sand stretched ahead of them, and in the distance were the rolling sand dunes. Chloe stared at them. These dunes were higher than the ones she'd seen before, all different shades of yellow, gold and orange, sculpted into gentle waves by the wind.

"Let's go!" Mina cried. Flicker gave a playful buck before leaping into a gallop, her heels kicking up the soft sand.

Chloe grabbed the pommel of her saddle in case Flame bucked too!

"It's OK," Flame called. "I won't buck. Just sit nice and still."

Then she tossed her head and galloped after Flicker. Soon she was going faster than Chloe had ever been in her life. She twisted her fingers in Flame's mane and clung on tightly.

"Don't . . . worry!" Flame puffed. "You

won't . . . fall off. Just . . . relax. Put your weight . . . into your stirrups."

Chloe did as Flame said, and to her surprise she found that she felt much safer in the saddle. She laughed out loud as the wind whipped through her hair and sand flew up around her. She remembered her blue kerchief and pulled it up over her mouth to keep out the gritty bits of sand.

The girls raced side by side until a little clump of palm trees came into sight. There were two other ponies there already, one grey and one black.

Mina slowed Flicker to a canter and then a trot. "That's Hanna and her pony, Ebony," she said to Chloe. "And Hanna's brother Abdou, with Cloud."

As they got closer, Chloe saw that the black pony had a pretty white blaze. Hanna was standing beside him, holding his bridle. Chloe slowed Flame to a walk behind Flicker and they made their way around the clump of palm trees. A young boy with imp-ish brown eyes was holding the grey pony's reins. When he saw Mina, he handed the reins to Hanna and ran towards them with a big smile on his face.

"Hi, Mina!" he called. "Are you ready for the pageant?"

Mina stopped and smiled at the boy. "Hi, Abdou," she said. She swivelled around in her saddle to look back at Chloe. "This is Hanna's little brother. Abdou, this is my friend Chloe."

Abdou fished in his pocket. "Hello, Chloe," he said. He pulled out a packet of sunflower seeds and held it up to her. "Would you like some sunflower seeds?"

"Where did you get those?" Mina gasped.

Abdou looked puzzled. "Hanna gave them to me," he said. "She bought them in the market yesterday."

Chloe stared at Mina in dismay. Surely *Hanna* couldn't have locked them in the stable last night! "No, thank you, Abdou," Chloe said. "You keep the seeds for yourself. We've just had breakfast."

As they rode on towards Hanna, Chloe hoped that they were wrong. "Surely Mina's best friend couldn't do such horrible things to her!" she whispered to Flame. She followed as Mina slid down from Flicker's back and led her towards the black pony.

"Hello, Hanna," Mina said, sounding slightly nervous. "Your mum said we'd find you here."

Hanna shrugged. "I'm surprised you bothered looking for me," she said. "You didn't come over last night, even though you said you would follow me after filling your water jug."

"I'm sorry, Hanna," Mina said, looking very upset. "When I got home we found that my saddlecloth had been ruined. So we had to spend hours and hours making another one. And then someone locked us in the stable!"

Hanna looked at the ground and said nothing.

"We wanted you to help us find out who did it," Mina went on. "We found sunflower seeds outside the stable . . . but then . . . we just met Abdou and he was eating a packet of them and he said . . . " She trailed off.

When Hanna looked up, her eyes were full of tears. "I didn't touch your saddle-cloth!" she burst out. "I promise I didn't!"

"I didn't say you did," Mina said in surprise. Chloe held up her hand, warning Mina to stop talking. She had a feeling Hanna had more to say.

One big, fat tear rolled down Hanna's cheek. "I didn't spoil your saddlecloth, but I *did* lock you in the stable. I came over to find you last night and I brought the sunflower seeds as a present. But you and Chloe were asleep on the hay. I was so jealous that I locked you both in the stable."

Mina looked bewildered. "Jealous of what?" she said.

"You and Chloe, of course!" said Hanna. "You're always making new friends! Nadia and Amira have been playing with us all the time recently, and now Chloe is helping you with the saddlecloth for the pageant. Sometimes I think you don't like me at all."

Mina threw her arms around her friend. "Of course I like you!"

"I don't know why," Hanna sniffed. "I'm too shy to make friends the way you do. I end up feeling left out all the time."

Mina looked amazed.

"You were right, Flame," Chloe whispered. "You thought she might be feeling left out."

"Yes," Flame agreed. "I don't think she

meant any real harm. She's obviously very sorry about locking the stable door."

Chloe stepped forward. "Mina told me that you like detective stories, Hanna. We still don't know who ruined her saddlecloth. Will you help us to find out?"

Hanna hesitated. "You mean you don't mind about what I did?"

"Let's forget about it," Mina said. "Chloe got us out with her lucky hairgrip. But you won't do anything like that again, will you?"

"Of course not," Hanna said firmly.

"Well then, that's fine," said Mina, linking her arm through her friend's. "We'll always be best friends, I promise."

Hanna smiled. "Good," she said. "I'm really sorry about locking the stable door."

She turned to Chloe. "I'm glad you had your lucky hairgrip with you."

Chloe smiled back. Hanna had been silly and selfish, but it looked as if Mina had forgiven her.

"Come on," said Mina. "We'd better get back into town if we're going to find out who *did* ruin my saddlecloth!"

7. Pretty at the Pageant

The girls trotted back across the dunes with Abdou and Cloud following them. They were trying to figure out how to discover the culprit.

"Maybe there are some clues on the saddlecloth," Hanna suggested.

"Clues?" Mina echoed. "It's totally ruined. How could there be any clues?"

But Chloe agreed with Hanna. "Detectives look for tiny traces of evidence," she said. "I think Hanna's right. We should take a closer look at it!"

69

"I guess so," Mina said thoughtfully.

They made their way to Mina's house and took the ponies into the stable, where they showed Hanna the ruined saddlecloth.

Hanna frowned. "It doesn't look as though the threads have been cut," she said, turning the cloth over in her hands. "It looks as if they've been scratched or picked loose with something sharp."

Chloe peered over her shoulder. "And are those black hairs clinging to the silk?" She pointed.

Mina looked at Hanna. "That's definitely a clue! Who do we know with short black hair?"

Chloe inspected the hairs more closely. "I don't think these are human hairs," she said. "But I think I know what they are . . ."

"*Cat* hairs!" Hanna exclaimed. "Of course!"

Suddenly, Flame gave a whinny, and Chloe turned to see what she wanted. Mina's black cat was curled up in the hay store, fast asleep.

"Let's have a look at his claws," said Chloe. "There could be evidence on them!"

She stroked the cat's head and then picked him up. Hanna took hold of his front paws and peered at them. "Look!" she said. "There are tiny bits of silver thread caught in the claws!"

"Pasha, you *naughty* cat!" Mina scolded.

Pasha gave a loud miaow and wriggled

71

out of Chloe's hands. Then he stalked out of the stable with his tail held high.

Mina smiled broadly. "I know Pasha didn't mean to upset me," she said. She gave Hanna a hug, then Chloe. "Thank you so much for helping me, both of you!"

Chloe blushed. "Well, I'm just happy that we're going to the pageant after all," she said. "But we'd better hurry up, or we'll be late!"

"I'll fetch my saddlecloth," Hanna said. "We can all get ready together!"

Mina fetched her grooming kit so she and Chloe could comb Flame and Flicker's lovely manes and tails. Hanna came back with Ebony and they oiled the ponies' hoofs and checked their saddlecloths to make sure they were straight.

"I think we're done," Mina said, giving Flicker a final pat.

Suddenly Chloe remembered something. "The ribbons!" she cried. She ran into the tack room to fetch the bag of ribbons. There were lots of different colours and she laid them out to see which would suit each pony.

"Blue and yellow for Flicker," she decided. "Red and gold for Flame." She looked at Ebony, whose saddlecloth was a lovely olive-green colour with silver tassels. "And silver ribbons for Ebony!"

Chloe had never plaited manes so fast in all her life, but she concentrated hard, weaving the ribbons in as she went.

"Our ponies have never looked so beautiful," Hanna declared. "Thank you, Chloe!"

The pageant took place just outside the town. As the three girls rode through the streets, Mina told Chloe about the races that took place each year.

"Everyone who has a pony joins in the pageant before the start of the race," she explained. "It's really good fun. Everyone who doesn't have a pony comes along to watch! Once the pageant is over, there are lots of exciting races. The fastest horses from all over the desert join in."

Chloe felt her stomach flip over in excitement. This adventure just got better and better!

The girls made their way to the starting point for the pageant. Chloe looked around at all the other ponies. They had pretty faces, just like Flame's, and they all had spectacular saddlecloths and bridles. Some of the riders wore flowing fabric head-dresses over their long embroidered gowns.

Chloe noticed that one man was walking around looking closely at the riders. Then he stopped to talk to another man. They looked up and pointed straight at Chloe and her friends.

"Those men are talking about us," Chloe said to Mina and Hanna.

One of the men came over.

"Hello there!" he called. "You have the prettiest ponies here. Would you like to lead the procession?"

"Lead the procession?" Mina squealed. She looked at Chloe and Hanna, who both grinned in delight. "We'd *love* to!"

The man showed them where to go. "Let the pageant begin!" he called, with a wave of his hand. Chloe nudged her heels against

Flame's side, and her pony walked forward
with her neck arched proudly. Flicker and
Ebony walked beside them, looking just as
beautiful. The route was lined with people,
and a huge cheer went up as they trotted
past.

"I can't believe it," Chloe murmured.

Flame tossed her head. "Oh, *I* can," she
said. "You've made us look magnificent."

Chloe beamed until her cheeks ached.
She felt as if she was going to burst with
pride!

As they reached the end of the procession, Chloe gazed around her at the
colourful scene. She noticed that the dunes
in the distance were beginning to shimmer,
and the swirls of sand were turning pink
and glittery . . .

"I think it's time for us to go," said Flame.

Chloe looked at Mina and Hanna. They
were surrounded by their friends who were
congratulating them. No one would notice
if she and Flame slipped away.

Quickly she trotted Flame away from the
crowds. As they drew near the dunes, a gust
of wind lifted little piles of sand that swirled
around Flame's hoofs.

Chloe gazed around at the desert one last
time. She wanted to remember this adventure forever.

Flame speeded up until she was galloping over the sand, but Chloe didn't need to hang on to her mane now. Flame had helped her become a much better rider, and she felt a lot braver.

The last of the sparkles disappeared, and Chloe looked down. Instead of a real golden mane she saw a glossy wooden neck. Flame was a carousel pony again, rising and falling smoothly as the carousel slowed to a halt. Chloe's blue cotton gown had vanished and she was wearing her cardigan and her denim skirt again.

"Did you enjoy your ride, Chloe?" asked a voice.

It was her dad, waving from the bottom of the steps that led up to the carousel.

Chloe waved back and slid down from the saddle.

"Goodbye, Flame," she whispered sadly, patting the pony's golden neck.

As she turned to go, she noticed something poking out of the pocket of her pink cardigan. "That's funny!" she said. She put her hand into her pocket.

With a gasp of delight, she pulled out the red and gold ribbons that had been woven into Flame's mane.

"Now I'll definitely remember my adventure forever!" she laughed.

She glanced back at Flame one last time and was sure she could see a twinkle in her lovely brown eyes.

Magic Pony Carousel

Sparkle

Poppy Shire

This was the most ride amazing Megan had ever been on! She tried to grip the pole tighter, then stared in surprise. She wasn't holding the pole. She was holding Sparkle's mane, and there was silky hair between her fingers, as if it was a real mane. She let go with one hand and stroked Sparkle's neck. It felt soft and warm. And then she heard the rhythm of horses' hoofs . . .

Megan gasped. What had happened to her carousel pony? The pink and silver sparkles began to fade away . . .

She was riding a real pony in a circus ring!

Brightheart

Poppy Shire

What was happening?

With a jolt, Brightheart's hoofs thudded against the ground. Amy grabbed hold of the front of the saddle. The bump shook away the last of the silvery sparkles that had been whirling around her head. She straightened up, puzzled.

Was this part of the carousel ride?

Then she gasped out loud.

She was riding a real live pony!

Brightheart's dark coat was no longer painted on. He had a jingling green leather bridle and a thick black mane . . .

But where were they? Amy turned around and nearly fell off Brightheart in surprise. A huge castle loomed up behind her.

Magic Pony Carousel

Star

Poppy Shire

The carousel music grew louder and the horses swooped through the air as they gathered speed. The breeze blew on Laura's cheeks and the fairground lights seemed to glitter and twinkle around her. To her surprise the breeze felt warm, like on a summer's day, and the air began to glow and shimmer like summery mist. She looked up and gasped. It was no longer a cool autumn evening – instead the sky was a beautiful bright blue, with the sun blazing down. And she wasn't holding on to the golden pole any more. She had real leather reins in one hand and a rope lasso in the other!

Jewel

Poppy Shire

The sparkly mist cleared away, leaving Sophie and Jewel standing alone in the darkness at a crossroads on a grassy heath. Sophie looked around, feeling utterly bewildered. A minute ago she'd been at a noisy, colourful fairground – and now she was in the middle of nowhere, in the middle of the night! She patted Jewel's wooden neck for comfort.

To her amazement, he snorted and shook his head. Jewel wasn't wooden at all! He was a real pony. Sophie stroked his thick, warm mane, and he reached his head round to nuzzle at her hand.

"What's going on?" Sophie breathed. "Where are we?"

Crystal

Poppy Shire

The carousel began to spin faster, and the fairground became a blur of laughing faces. Everything started to disappear in a rainbow mist. Emily blinked. She wanted to rub her eyes, but they were going so fast, she didn't dare let go of Crystal's reins. Silvery sparkles whirled around her, and the rainbow colours of the fairground changed to dazzling white. Everything shone and glittered with light, and Emily gasped out loud. This wasn't the fairground any more. She and Crystal were in the middle of a snowstorm!

The prices shown below are correct at the time of going to press. However, Macmillan Publishers reserves the right to show new retail prices on covers, which may differ from those previously advertised.

Magic Pony Carousel:

Sparkle	ISBN-13: 978-0-330-44041-7	£3.99
	ISBN-10: 0-330-44041-1	
Brightheart	ISBN-13: 978-0-330-44042-4	£3.99
	ISBN-10: 0-330-44042-X	
Star	ISBN-13: 978-0-330-44043-1	£3.99
	ISBN-10: 0-330-44043-8	
Jewel	ISBN-13: 978-0-330-44044-8	£3.99
	ISBN-10: 0-330-44044-6	
Crystal	ISBN-13: 978-0-330-44597-9	£3.99
	ISBN-10: 0-330-44597-9	
Flame	ISBN-13: 978-0-330-44598-6	£3.99
	ISBN-10: 0-330-44598-7	

All Pan Macmillan titles can be ordered from our website, www.panmacmillan.com, or from your local bookshop and are also available by post from:

Bookpost, PO Box 29, Douglas, Isle of Man IM99 1BQ
Credit cards accepted. For details:
Telephone: 01624 677237
Fax: 01624 670923
Email: bookshop@enterprise.net
www.bookpost.co.uk